PEPPER BELLE

*To my very good friend
Dr. Nick Portman

Willie J. Ferrero*

PEPPER BELLE

Willie J. Ferrero

Copyright © 2002 by Willie J. Ferrero.

Library of Congress Number: 2002092599
ISBN: Hardcover   1-4010-6265-2
                Softcover   1-4010-6264-4

All rights reserved. No part of this book may be reproduced or transmitted in any form or by any means, electronic or mechanical, including photocopying, recording, or by any information storage and retrieval system, without permission in writing from the copyright owner.

This is a work of fiction. Names, characters, places and incidents either are the product of the author's imagination or are used fictitiously, and any resemblance to any actual persons, living or dead, events, or locales is entirely coincidental.

Sketches drawn by Alex and Dan Brennan

This book was printed in the United States of America.

To order additional copies of this book, contact:
Xlibris Corporation
1-888-795-4274
www.Xlibris.com
Orders@Xlibris.com
15611-FERR

This is a story based on fact and fiction. It takes place in the small town of East Longmeadow, Massachusetts. The story follows the birth of Pepper Belle, a Standardbred race horse and the early life of Betsy Verini. The events depict the onset of Tourette Syndrome in both Betsy and Pepper Belle and how it created a touching life for both.

"Anything, any signs yet?" Willie yelled to Big John from the bedroom. Big John, Willie's son, was watching TV in the family room. Next to the regular TV was another, smaller monitor screen which showed the events in the foaling barn. A video camera connected to the monitor kept a 24 hour watch of Cool Pat as she awaited the birth of her, now overdue, foal. John told his father that nothing was happening yet.

The Ferrero's Farm, home of the Masconette Stable, was the perfect place for people, horses, and most other living things. The property straddled the crest of a hill. The ranch style house was set way back from the road. The huge front yard was a large expanse of lawn scattered with both maple and oak trees. A long driveway swept from the far end of the property past the foaling barn with adjacent paddock on up to the house. At the edge of the foaling paddock, the driveway split and also went off toward the main barn and private training track. The barn housing the horse stalls was set a few hundred feet behind the house. Between house and barn was another expanse of large trees scattered about the lawn. On the opposite side of the property from the foaling barn lay the training track.

Horses don't usually have problems foaling, but concern was

beginning to grow because Cool Pat was about 30 days overdue. John and his dad took turns during the nights watching the mare. During one of Willie's watches he fell asleep in his leather chair. His last observance at about 3:30 AM showed Cool Pat walking around picking on bits of hay but with no apparent physical signs that precede birth. John woke up around 6 AM, went to the family room and shouted to his sleeping dad.

"Dad! There's something dark in the straw. It looks like the foal." A clear view was not available because of the location of the camera. Both ran out to the barn and there stood Cool Pat licking her new foal. John and Willie went about checking Cool Pat and washing her. She had just passed the afterbirth. The foal's navel was cleaned with iodine and trimmed.

By this time Peggy, Willie's wife, came out to the barn. She had seen a lot of births over the years but was just as excited as the first one. "Is it a boy or a girl?" Peggy asked. "It's a little filly, Mom," replied Willie.

Just about then the foal finally made it to her feet and was poking around her mother's milk bag. In a few minutes she latched on and started suckling. This is important because the first milk has Colostrum, which a foal needs to develop its immune system. She was still wobbly but managed to smell the four stall walls, Willie and John. Mom came inside the stall to make sure they did a good job rubbing and drying the foal.

Inside of an hour she was bouncing around the stall driving Cool Pat crazy by butting her stomach trying for more milk. When she got over the rambunctiousness, Cool Pat would lift up her leg and give a slight kick-like motion or push her with her nose, kind of reprimanding her baby for bad manners. It was fun to watch. The foal grew stronger by the minute. A call had been made to Dr. W. O'Leary, the farm vet from Granby, Connecticut. He arrived at about 9:30 AM and examined the foal and mother. Everything was just fine. The foal got her first shots.

Cool Pat and the new foal

By this time everyone was hungry and they all went to the house for breakfast. Some of the excitement had worn off and things began to get back to normal in the Ferrero household.

During the early afternoon John decided to let the mare and foal out in the sunny 100' x 100' white boarded paddock, connected to the foaling barn. Cool Pat was reluctant to go out and was very protective of her baby, as well she should be. John gently pushed the foal out on the mowed green grass and Cool Pat came crashing out to protect her foal. The mare and foal romped side by side around and around. When things slowed down, the foal laid down in the sunny green paddock to rest, her mother standing over her.

Down the street, less than 1/4 mile away, lived the Verini family. They were the Ferrero's closest neighbors. To the rear of the Verini homestead was a dirt road that connected to the Ferrero place and led to a quarry lake about 3/4 miles away. The road was rather overgrown with high grass and clusters of blueberry bushes. Nature blessed the area with an abundance of birds and furred animals. In days gone by, the road was used to move brownstones from the quarry to the cutting barns. It now served as a private roadway for the two neighbors.

Bob and Mary Verini had an eleven year old daughter. Her name was Elizabeth, but everyone called her Betsy. She was a pretty girl with a thick mass of wavy, chestnut colored hair and huge, soft brown eyes. She was intelligent and kind, with a winning personality. She was just as comfortable with adults as she was with her friends. She was even more comfortable with animals.

Betsy Verini

Betsy loved to go to the Ferrero barn and hang out with the horses and Big John's huge German Shepherd named Arnie. The red and white barn was a wonderful place. In addition to the horses there were always cats and often a new litter of kittens. Either Willie or Big John always seemed to be there doing one chore or another. Mary Verini would call Big John or Peggy to find out if it was okay for Betsy to come over. This became such a daily ritual that Peggy told Mary that Betsy had a standing invitation and could come over anytime. Exuberantly, Betsy would run down the grassy dirt road. "Hi, Big John or Hi Mr. F.," she would sing out as she played with Arnie and headed toward the horse barn.

Today all the excitement was doubled. Peggy called Mary and told her of Cool Pat's foaling. When Betsy heard this, she couldn't get out of her school clothes fast enough. She ran all the way down the road to the foaling barn paddock. A few minutes later, Mary arrived as well.

She stopped in the house and then she and Peggy followed Betsy.

Big John and Arnie ran to the paddock as Betsy was going right through the rails. Any other time this wouldn't have been a problem but Big John was concerned that maybe Cool Pat might be too protective and kick Betsy. He didn't need to worry. Cool Pat was so used to Betsy being around, bringing her carrots and being her friend, that she just showed off her baby. She was also looking for the carrot Betsy had forgotten in all her excitement.

The foal took an immediate liking to her as well. Betsy would pet and rub the foal under the watchful eye of Cool Pat. It didn't take many days before the foal would recognize Betsy and come right to her. Betsy would stay every afternoon until suppertime, and would usually arrive at about 7:30 AM on Saturdays.

When two weeks had passed, the foal was running and jumping like a deer. Willie decided it was time to take Cool Pat out of the paddock on a lead shank and grass her on the big lawn in front of the homestead. The mare followed Willie out of the paddock nickering to the foal to follow her. The foal was a little confused and hesitated, causing Cool Pat to spin around, whinnying and in general, making a big fuss. Arnie started barking at the foal in an effort to get her out of the gate. Cool Pat, thinking her baby was in trouble, began rearing up until all of a sudden, the foal ran through the open gate. The foal nestled up to her mother and drank some milk. Things settled down and the mare started eating the lush green grass, while the foal took great delight in running in huge circles before coming back to the mare.

The foal grew quickly, got stronger and faster and would run further and further away before returning for something to eat. As long as the mare could see her baby, everything was okay. One time the foal's curiosity carried her in back of the homestead. Cool Pat became very upset, whinnying one time after another like a human mother would call a lost child. She frantically ran around Willie in a circle calling her foal. The foal, preoccupied with a Monarch butterfly perched on a rose bush, didn't really care until Arnie became upset and started barking and running around the foal. Then panic seemed to set in, the foal's tail stood up straight as if it were starched and she bolted around the house looking for her mother. As time passed it all became routine, and Cool Pat was less perturbed as she got used to the idea that her foal was exploring. At times when Betsy was there she would try to chase the foal, but was no match for her. The foal would run out in a circle, then run right at Betsy swerving to the left or right at the last minute. Betsy came to appreciate this playfulness. When they both were exhausted, they would lay down in the shade of the tall, stately Maple and Oak trees.

The foal and the butterfly

The bond between Betsy and the foal grew. Betsy started wondering when the foal would be named. Everyone began making suggestions, none of which seemed to fit. Betsy remarked about the foal being a lady and maybe Belle of the Ball after a character in a story she had read in school. Willie cited how feisty and peppery she acted. Willie suggested that they call her Pepper for her antics and Belle because she was a lady. Everyone jumped on the idea and the foal was named Pepper Belle.

School summer vacation soon came and Betsy hardly missed a day with Pepper Belle. Each day she would bring tidbits for Pepper Belle and could not wait until Big John or Willie would take Cool Pat out front for grass. Pepper and Betsy would start rough housing with one another and then they would tire. Pepper would get a snack from Cool Pat. Betsy could always depend on finding cookies or fruit on the front porch table. Then both would lay down to rest in the cool shade.

As summer came to near end, both horse and little girl grew. Leaves were showing their autumn splendor. The usual warm days and cool evenings started Pepper's winter coat growing. Betsy got all new school clothes. She had to go to the Ferreros to show Peg and Pepper Belle.

Betsy went back to school. For her turn at Show and Tell, Betsy brought in her pictures of Pepper Belle. She proudly told about her experience running, petting and playing with her best friend. Her girl friends wanted to come see Pepper Belle. She told them she would ask the Ferreros if she could invite some friends to see Pepper Belle.

The ending school bell couldn't come fast enough, but when it did, Betsy was the first one out. When she got to the Ferreros, she was yelling. "Can I bring my friends? Can I bring my friends to see Pepper Belle?"

"Sure, why not," replied Big John. "This weekend will be okay." When Betsy told her friends the next day at school, it seemed like the entire class took on the air of excited anticipation.

Betsy shows off her new school clothes.

The following Saturday, several cars drove up to the Ferrero's Masconette Farm. There were seven girls and two boys with either their mother or father. All were class friends of Betsy's. As usual, Betsy was already there at 7:30 AM and greeted everyone. Names were exchanged and everyone went off to the barn, Arnie and Betsy leading the way. How proud she was to show off her best friend, Pepper Belle. The foal was shining in the sun as Betsy let her in the paddock with Cool Pat. Of course, Betsy had spent an hour brushing and rubbing the two. Betsy's friends were amazed by her lack of fear of Cool Pat, who was a very large animal. "Woof, woof, woof," Betsy shouted. The kids and everyone laughed because Arnie the dog woofed right back. Everyone took turns petting the foal and wishing they had a horse.

Big John was getting ready to jog Rain Reign Rein and was about to hitch the horse to the cart as everyone came running from the foaling barn. Betsy had been given rides on the sulky before, and yelled, "Big John! Can I have a ride?" John was big hearted and found it hard to say no, especially to Betsy. He enjoyed the excitement of kids when they went around the private 1/2 mile track. After watching Betsy go around a few times, all the kids wanted rides. Big John, not wanting to disappoint anyone, spent an hour giving all nine kids a ride.

The adults laughed, talked and remarked that the kids "wouldn't forget this day." After everyone left, Betsy pleaded with Willie to take Cool Pat out so Pepper Belle could run around and play. Being late Saturday afternoon, Willie said that Peggy was probably getting ready to go to church as Mass was at 5:30 PM. Betsy pleaded her case until Willie gave in. "I guess we can go Sunday morning," he said. Out came Cool Pat and right at her side bounded Pepper Belle. After being cooped up in the small paddock, Pepper had a reserve of unspent energy and she was determined to let it all out. Up and down the hill, around the house, down to the barn again and again. Betsy woofed, woofed, and woofed as she watched her buddy fly by. "You sound like Arnie," Willie said to Betsy. "I don't mean to" she replied.

Willie said, "Oh, that's okay." He thought it was cute. He never realized it was the first sign of trouble.

Soon the brilliant New England foliage peaked and Thanksgiving Day passed. School for Betsy brought new experiences, many of them not good. Every once in a while Betsy would woof, woof, woof. At first, it was funny, everyone laughed. A few more times and her teacher asked her to please refrain from "fooling around." Betsy agreed, and the class continued on and the day ended with no further interruption. The incident bothered Betsy, however. She couldn't understand why she was doing this. She didn't mean to or even think about doing the woofing, it just seemed to happen even though she didn't want it to.

Unfortunately, try as she might, she couldn't stop it. Her teacher became irritated and started to scold Betsy and demanded that she stop interrupting the class. Betsy now became very conscious of her problem. No one understood that she couldn't control her woofing. Some of the other students started calling her names such as "Woofy," "Woof Girl," or simply "Dumb-Dumb." The incessant whispering behind her back began to work on Betsy's emotions and personality.

Betsy's mother and father began to worry about her behavior, especially when the school principal threatened expulsion if she didn't stop her "foolishness." Her parents were sympathetic and this helped but was inadequate. Betsy became very quiet and introverted. Her school grades dropped badly, she lost her happy outgoing personality. She wanted to spend more time at her only sanctuary, the Ferrero's barn with what was beginning to seem like her only friend, Pepper Belle.

Big John, Willie and Peggy could see the changes and offered support as best they could. However, they really didn't know what to do. No one knew what was wrong. Betsy would spend hours with Pepper, talking to her in soft tones as she rubbed her neck or head.

Betsy tells Pepper about the kids at school.

It seemed like Betsy's only relief was when she was alone with Pepper. The only time you ever saw a semblance of Betsy's old smile would be when Pepper did some stupid thing like rear up or chase her tail like a dog would do. Kids at school had their fun by tormenting Betsy with crudely drawn pictures on the black board, or tormenting her with woofs, calling her crazy and worse yet, "cookoo dog."

Betsy didn't want to go to school. With all the trouble, her parents didn't have the heart to make her go. Mary and Bob were at their wit's end when a school nurse suggested they seek help from their family doctor. Dr. Smyth gave Betsy a complete examination, taking both blood and urine tests. He could find nothing wrong. His suggestion was to see a psychologist for further testing. Bob and Mary agreed. Dr. Smyth made Betsy an appointment for an examination and evaluation. After several visits the psychologist started to suspect the cause might be neurological.

He suggested that the Verinis take Betsy to a neurologist. They had no other choice, although the very idea of taking Betsy to a neurologist made them nervous. Things were only getting worse for Betsy and they needed some answers. Dr. Harvey recommended Dr. Lassaby. The Verinis scheduled an appointment with him for the following week.

Meanwhile, the school notified Betsy's parents that if she didn't go back to school she would be held back a grade. A sorry day for Betsy started when she got on the bus for school Monday morning. She had learned to sit up front next to the bus driver to avoid some of the kids picking on her. Sitting next to the driver was the new bus monitor, named Mrs. Harris. Mrs. Harris lived next to one of Betsy's old "used to be friends."

When she saw Betsy, she said in a low tone to the bus driver, "Is this the cookoo Woof girl the kids all talk about?" Betsy wasn't supposed to hear but she did. She started to cry profusely and kept asking the bus driver " Please take me home, please take me home."

The bus driver was irritated with Mrs. Harris and let her know about it with a few choice words and facial expressions. The bus arrived at school and the kids all started getting out. All except Betsy, cringing in the corner of her seat crying, "Please take me home. Please." Mrs. Harris kept order as the kids left. She then tried to comfort Betsy. Betsy would have no part of her. The bus driver sent Mrs. Harris to the office so they could call Betsy's mother.

When Mary arrived, Betsy was sobbing and trembling. "Mom, please take me home, please take me home. I don't want to go to school, everyone hates me." She was sobbing deeply, hanging on to her mother's waist. Mary had never seen her daughter in such a state and shook trying to contain how upset she was. She noticed that Betsy seemed more upset by Mrs. Harris than anything else and asked her to get off the bus. Once she had gone, the bus driver pulled Mary aside. She told Mary that he thought Betsy must have overheard the cruel comment Mrs. Harris had made. Now, Mary was shaking with anger. She took Betsy to the car where they could both regain their composure before going into school. Mary held Betsy and felt her deep sobs. When the body wrenching crying did not dissipate, she decided to take her home and call the school from there.

Once they were home and Betsy was somewhat calmer, Mary went to her room, closed the door, and picked up the phone. As soon as Mary called she was put through to the principal, Mr. Lewis. She repeated what the bus driver had told her. He had already heard the story. She informed him that she never wanted to see Mrs. Harris on a school bus again.

To make a trying week that much more difficult, the mother of Betsy's "best friend," Sue, called Mary. She told her that Betsy was not going to be invited to Sue's birthday party. She said that Sue was afraid Betsy would be embarrassed when she woofed and the other kids would make fun of her. The truth be known, Sue didn't want her there. Betsy withdrew further and further. The one exception was in her relationship with Pepper. She wanted to go see and talk to Pepper Belle. After all, Pepper didn't make fun of her and she felt at peace in the barn with her, even when she woofed.

Both Bob and Mary went to the neurologist appointment with Betsy. When their turn came, Dr. Lassaby welcomed the Verinis into his office. He directed Bob and Mary to take chairs at his desk. He led Betsy to a couch in the far corner of his office. Around the couch and on a low, round coffee table in front of it were scattered books, toys, games and puzzles. He sat down with Betsy and told her that he wanted to talk to her parents for a few minutes and that she was free to read or find something that interested her.

He sat down at his desk with Bob and Mary and asked them why they were there. Between the two of them, it all spilled out in a flood. He had reports from Drs. Smyth and Harvey, so he knew the story from a strictly medical perspective. He wanted the picture filled in. He had a hunch. He began asking them questions, all the while with one eye on Betsy. Some of the questions seemed odd even though the answers were generally in the affirmative. He asked if Betsy spoke words out of context, if she made noises other than "woof," if she kicked unexpectedly, if she pulled on her clothes.

As Mary was describing how Betsy pulled on her left sleeve with her right hand, he was observing the behavior. Betsy was sitting with a book in her lap, obviously not reading it. Mary told him that she thought it was caused by nervousness brought on by all the pressure she was under. Dr. Lassaby went over to Betsy and performed some reflex tests. Betsy woofed and became visibly uneasy. He thanked her for putting up with him and returned to her parents.

"From what I understand from you, what I've observed today and what I know from the other doctors' reports, I think Betsy may have Tourette Syndrome," Dr. Lassaby told them.

"What the heck is that?" Bob blurted out.

The Verinis visit Doctor Lassaby's office.

Dr. Lassaby provided them with a brief, overall description of Tourette Syndrome. He told them that the woofing and sleeve pulling were symptoms called "tics." He then explained that his niece had been diagnosed with it a year before. He had done some research. As it turned out, the Verinis had been fortunate to have had Dr. Lassaby recommended to them. Many doctors are unaware of the symptoms of Tourette's. Some of them have never even heard of it.

He asked that they make another appointment for Betsy so he could run some tests. He wanted to have an opportunity for further evaluation and he hoped that Betsy would become more at ease with him.

Betsy's parents were asked to gather some information. He wrote down several things he wanted them to do or keep track of. Mary looked at the paper. He wanted to know how frequently each tic occurred. He asked them to make note if a certain situation seemed to increase the frequency. He asked them to detail any family school or other personal problems. In addition, they were asked to have the school evaluate Betsy for various learning disabilities. The information would help the doctor complete his evaluation.

With far more questions than answers, the Verinis went home. When they arrived, Betsy's first request was to go see Pepper Belle. Even though it was a little late, Mary called the Ferreros. Big John answered and immediately asked how the doctor's visit had gone. Mary told him what had transpired. Big John was an exceptionally understanding man. He told Mary he would watch for Betsy down the road and then make sure she got home safe later. He went out to the road to look for her. As soon as he saw her he was again struck by the change that had come over her. Betsy was no longer the happy-go-lucky girl that used to skip to the barn. Big John turned the lights on in the barn and tried to spark a smile from Betsy with one of his corny jokes while they walked to Pepper's stall. Nothing John could do would crack the somber, quiet, dead pan look on her face.

When John opened the stall door Pepper's face was right there and she practically gave Betsy a slobbering kiss. This brought a smile to Betsy's face. The telephone was ringing in the main barn and Big John went to answer it. Betsy put her arm around Pepper's neck and for a few moments it seemed like time stood still. You would think Pepper knew what was going on. She nuzzled Betsy in the stomach trying to bite the buckle on her belt, then started to lip her hair.

Betsy went to get Pepper some fresh hay, closing the stall door behind her. When she returned a few moments later, she thought Pepper was putting on a show for her. It seemed she had gone wild. Around the huge stall she ran bucking, kicking and squeaking under the watchful eye of Cool Pat. The squeaking broke up Betsy into laughter, and anyone could see Betsy's torment momentarily gone. When Big John came back, he found Betsy hugging Pepper Belle and saying, "I love you. I love you."

Big John wiped his eyes, made some noise, and then called to Betsy, "Are you ready to go home?"

"No. Big John, can I sleep here?"

"What do you mean, sleep here?" said John.

"I want to sleep in the straw with Pepper."

"No, I don't think that would work out, but you know that you can come back tomorrow."

Hearing this, Betsy seemed to shrink and her smile vanished instantly. John, walking her home, tried to lift her spirits. "Saturday I'll give you a ride on the sulky with Rain Reign Rein."

"Okay," said Betsy with little emotion. Mary met them at the door. Betsy thanked Big John for letting her come over so late, and then she turned and ran to her bedroom. Big John and Mary spoke for a while discussing how to handle some of the problems. Both agreed that Betsy should be treated gently, and that seeing Pepper would help since she was at ease with her.

Pepper bucking and squealing

In two months summer vacation would be here again and not soon enough for Betsy. She endured school nowadays and was not looking forward to the experiences to come. School officials knew that Betsy had been diagnosed with Tourette Syndrome. Still not understanding the disorder, they believed that Betsy either simply lacked self control or was consciously causing trouble.

Betsy's classmate tormentors were persistent with their name calling and harassment. One day when she entered the classroom, she saw that someone had drawn a picture of a girl with a dog head on the blackboard captioned, "Betsy Woof Woof." Betsy was devastated. Although other teachers were sympathetic to her plight, her own teacher only made small, ineffective effort to curb the attacks. Betsy's tics worsened to the point where she was woofing and tugging on her sleeve many times each hour. One of the cruelest acts came when the janitor offered to build a large wooden box with a window in it so Betsy could sit in it and not disturb anyone. At last, her teacher's displeasure grew to a point where she wanted Betsy out of the classroom.

The pain was overpowering and Betsy sank deeper into depression. Never being asked to a party or asked to be on a sport team of any kind was torturous. No one should be treated like that. If it hadn't been for Betsy's daily visit with Pepper, Betsy would have been in much lower spirits than she was. Each day Betsy would take Pepper out and after a lot of rough housing and running, the two would settle down in the barn. Betsy would tell Pepper about the mean kids and what happened each day. She would woof and constantly tug her sleeve, but Pepper didn't care and never made fun of her; instead she would lip her ears and nuzzle her while pushing Betsy with her head. The two spent all possible time together and even Pepper showed signs of being sad when Betsy went to school.

Betsy went back to Dr. Lassaby's office. The Verinis brought all the documentation and information he had asked them for. He told them that he wanted to schedule her for a few tests. He spent a lot of time with Betsy, this time asking her various questions. By the time they left, Betsy felt comfortable with Dr. Lassaby. She wasn't even afraid of the tests she was going to have. He had explained them all to her. He then spent time with the whole family going into more depth about Tourette Syndrome.

By the time school let out in late June, Pepper had blossomed into a very desirable yearling. As was typical of her breed, she was a Bay. Her black mane and tail were thick and full. She was well conformed and bright eyed. It was now time to break Pepper to harness and cart. She was a Standardbred race horse and harness racing was part of her heritage.

Betsy's daily visits continued. Sometimes she even showed signs of being her old self, thanks to not having to go to school and being with Pepper Belle. She would watch intently as Pepper began her training. After Pepper learned the bit, she was quickly moved outside to learn the lines. Pepper was very smart and inside of a week she was hitched to a jog cart and started walking and jogging around the farm track. Big John even let Betsy ride on the jog cart with him. Of course, the excitement generated in Betsy was a fuel for laughter and good times.

By the time the summer ended, Betsy was looking better. The pleasant surroundings replenished and invigorated her. The fact that she wasn't being harassed on a daily basis improved her outlook even though she continued to woof and tug on her sleeve.

Pepper continued to improve in her conditioning. She was starting to develop leg muscles and her coat would glisten in the sun. Each day Big John would jog her for 30 minutes on the track, then give her a bath and turn her out in the paddock. Horses love to frolic in the paddock and Pepper showed that she was no different.

Big John jogging Pepper.

She seemed to be developing some odd behaviors, however. She would bite at her flanks and chase her tail as a puppy might do. Horses sometimes bite their flanks if they have colic or stomach problems. Pepper began to do this so often that Big John thought she might be suffering with colic, although Pepper never lost her appetite and had no trouble making manure.

After doing the usual things for a horse with colic to help them, Big John recognized that the remedies had no effect on Pepper. When more than a week passed without signs of improvement, Big John called Dr. O'Leary. John asked him to stop in when he was in the area. John had expressed no great urgency, emergencies kept coming up and it was five days before the Vet showed up. By then Pepper had started something new. For four days she had been kicking the stall walls incessantly. She also made weird noises not usually made by horses, high squeaky noises, almost like a baby crying.

Dr. O'Leary talked to Big John and Willie about treatment for Pepper. They decided to modify and continue the treatment for colic. Pepper was a racehorse and so they could use no drugs. Unfortunately, the modified treatment had no more effect on her than the initial treatment had.

Shortly after Dr. O'Leary started treating Pepper, he received a letter from Dr. Nick Dodman from Tufts University. He is one of the foremost animal behaviorists in the country. He is currently engaged in a study of horses who were exhibiting the symptoms of colic: spinning around, biting their flanks, and kicking their stalls, but who did not actually have colic. Dr. O'Leary knew that description fit Pepper Belle and brought the letter to the Ferreros for Willie to read.

By this time fall had fully set in. The ground was frozen and frequently covered with a layer of frost. Most of the leaves had dropped from the trees, although a few clung stubbornly to the gray limbs and branches. Small, puffy clouds hung in the crisp blue sky. It seemed as if there was always at least a breeze. Sometimes the breeze turned into a cold and bitter wind, blowing the fallen leaves around in cyclone-like circles in the air.

Willie called Dr. Dodman and spoke to his secretary. He explained that he had a horse which had colic symptoms without the colic. She asked him some questions about Pepper Belle. She was interested in knowing how old Pepper was, for how long she had exhibited the symptoms and the severity of them. She took Willie's address and phone number and told him that she would be getting back to him shortly. The next day a thick envelope appeared in the mailbox bearing the return address of Tufts University. Included was a letter from Dr. Dodman and a long questionnaire. The letter itself provided little more information than the letter which Dr. O'Leary had received. The questionnaire required Big John and Willie to describe Pepper Belle's symptoms in detail. They put their heads together and tried to remember every detail they could. As soon as it was complete, they sent it back to Dr. Dodman. The following day Dr. Dodman's office called and wanted to know when they could see Pepper Belle.

Big John and Willie were not crazy about letting Pepper Belle go. She was nearly ready to race. They talked about it and decided to deal with her as best they could and see how things went. By January the weather was bad and Pepper Belle was really not responding to any sort of treatment they had devised for her. Big John and Willie finally decided they really didn't have any other option than to bring her to Tufts.

Willie, Peggy and Big John trailered Pepper to Tufts. Dr. Dodman told them she would probably need to stay for five to six weeks. They would put her in a padded stall and she would be monitored 24 hours a day by video camera. Dr. Dodman explained that they would be running tests on Pepper to determine whether or not she had Tourette's Syndrome. They were stunned. During the drive home they talked it over and decided not to say anything yet to Betsy or her family.

Betsy had known Pepper was going to Tufts. She had had an

opportunity to say goodbye. Still, she was very distressed by the fact that Pepper was gone and continued to come over to the Ferreros nearly every day to hang out around the barn with Big John. Betsy would perk up some while she was there but without Pepper Belle, it was just not the same. The second week Pepper was gone Willie and Peggy decided to speak to Betsy's mom.

They walked over to the Verini's. Betsy's mom was getting dinner ready and Betsy was nowhere to be seen.

"How is she doing?" Peggy asked.

"The same and worse . . . since Pepper Belle's gone," replied Mary. She seemed very tired and kind of spiritless.

We were hoping you would let us take Betsy with us when we go to see Pepper on Saturday."

A wide smile brightened Mary's face.

"Of course! She would love it. She misses Pepper so much. I know it would do her a lot of good."

Willie and Peggy heard a tell-tale "woof" somewhere in the house and the three of them stood quietly for a minute.

"Would it be all right to tell her now? Mary asked.

"By all means," Willie and Peggy said in unison.

Her mother called her and Betsy shuffled into the kitchen with her head down, yanking at her sleeves. Mary winked at the Ferreros.

"Betsy, Peggy and Willie were wondering if you might like to go with them to Tufts on Saturday . . ." She didn't have the opportunity to finish because Betsy interrupted with a loud squeal of delight.

"Apparently she'd like to go," laughed Mary.

The week flew by and Saturday arrived, a crisp, clear sunny day. An extremely excited Betsy showed up very early. She was carrying a bag full of carrots, one of Pepper Belle's favorite treats. Betsy followed everyone around until it was time to leave.

Willie and Peggy talk to Mrs. Verini.

From the time they got into the car and for nearly the entire length of the Massachusetts Turnpike, Betsy could do nothing but talk about Pepper Belle. As they neared the end of their journey, Betsy's attention finally shifted to the world outside the car.

The landscape had changed from rolling hills and forests to tall buildings and concrete. Betsy was fascinated by all the buildings and signs they were passing. Tufts University is in North Grafton, Massachusetts, near Worcester. Betsy had never been this far east. She was used to the smaller city of Springfield near her home.

At last they reached the University and Willie found a place to park. Although Betsy was still very excited, she was a bit apprehensive as well. Everything seemed so much bigger than at home. They were greeted by Dr. Dodman. Willie and Peggy introduced Betsy to him. Dr. Dodman had a way with children as well as animals. He was so friendly to Betsy, ignoring the occasional "woof," that he was able to put her at ease.

On the way to see Pepper Belle the doctor gave her a tour. They even observed a couple of operations being performed on other horses. One was having a stomach operation and one was having its leg operated on. Seeing this, Betsy became somewhat nervous and upset. Dr. Dodman assured her that Pepper Belle would not be having any operations and this calmed her down considerably. They navigated the wide corridors and finally arrived at the stalls. Betsy saw Pepper looking through the bars of her stall and immediately big tears started rolling down her cheeks. She was so excited to see her friend.

The handler opened the stall door and stood for a moment in front of Pepper. She was a little concerned about Betsy getting close to Pepper. Her concern soon melted away as Betsy and Pepper Belle greeted each other. It seemed as if Pepper had been waiting for Betsy. She calmly nuzzled her as Betsy rubbed and petted Pepper's neck.

Betsy sat down on the straw, as comfortable as if she was sitting on a chair in her own living room. She opened the bag of carrots she had held onto the whole ride and began feeding them to Pepper. All the while, she spoke calmly and soothingly to her. Betsy told her not only how much she had missed her but also filled Pepper in on things that were happening around the barn at home, and what was going on in Betsy's own life. Both Dr. Dodman and the handler were amazed by the love and connection between girl and horse.

While Betsy and Pepper Belle became reacquainted, Willie and Dr. Dodman talked about Pepper. Several tests had already been done and more where scheduled. Although the results were not in yet from most of the tests, Dr. Dodman told Willie that he was fairly sure Pepper Belle had Tourette Syndrome. Even though Willie knew full well that that is what Pepper was being tested for, the news stunned him. Willie seemed so surprised and uncomprehending that Dr. Dodman launched into another explanation of the disease. Willie shook his head as if coming out of a fog and stopped the doctor mid-sentence. Willie quietly told Dr. Dodman all about Betsy. When Willie had finished, they both watched Betsy and Pepper Belle thoughtfully for a few minutes. Then it was time to leave.

Betsy got a little weepy as she hugged Pepper Belle's neck, telling her goodbye and promising to return the following week. She looked at Willie, who nodded. Betsy could definitely come again next week.

On the way home they stopped for lunch. Betsy didn't eat out very often and was a little nervous about it. In no time though, they were sitting at the table talking about her visit with Pepper Belle and she relaxed. Although she never stopped pulling on the sleeve of her blouse, she looked decidedly more happy . . . Betsy's visit had had a calming affect on her and she napped for a little while on the way home.

Pepper Belle greets Betsy at Tufts University.

They had decided not to say anything to Betsy about the possibility of Pepper having Tourette Syndrome until they were sure it was so. They also wanted to talk to Betsy's parents and determine how best to deal with it. Willie was not sure how she would feel about it.

The following weekend they made the trip again. Betsy was nearly as excited as she had been the week before. This time she brought Pepper a radio in addition to the carrots. There was usually a radio playing in the barn at home and Betsy thought it would give Pepper some company. At first, Dr. Dodman told Willie he wasn't sure whether or not Betsy would be able to leave the radio. He was afraid it might interfere with monitoring Pepper Belle. He spoke to the handler about it and then made a phone call. He found that if she put the radio on low, as far from the microphone as possible, there would be no trouble at all. Betsy was relieved and sniffed back the tears that had begun welling in her eyes. The handler assured Betsy she would play the radio for Pepper. Betsy was so happy that she hugged the handler and then gave Dr. Dodman a big hug. Dr. Dodman was British and as good as he was with children, he was still a bit "stuffy" about hugs and such. Betsy's hug seemed to knock some of the stuffing right out of him.

When Willie dropped Betsy off, he and Peggy went inside to speak to her parents. Betsy went off to her room, humming quietly and tugging her sleeve.

"I'd like to speak to you about Pepper Belle," Willie began.

Bob, Willie and Peggy sat down at the kitchen table. Mary was making tea. She served them each a cup and then joined them. Bob and Mary were apprehensive. Their worst fear was that something was seriously wrong with Pepper and that she would have to be put down. Each, in their own mind, was trying to figure out what effect that would have on Betsy.

"The doctor at Tufts University believes that Pepper Belle may have Tourette Syndrome. He has a few more tests to run and should be able to tell us for sure next week. Willie and Peggy waited to see what their reaction would be.

Bob and Mary looked at Willie and Peggy and then at each other with their mouths open and their jaws slack. They could not believe that the horse their little girl loved so much shared her disorder. Tears welled up in Mary's eyes as she felt relief that Pepper Belle would not have to be destroyed. Bob began to question Willie about what this meant to her career as a race horse. The conversation drifted back and forth between discussion of Pepper Belle and discussion of Betsy. Bob and Mary told the Ferreros that things had not gotten any better for her in school. Most mornings they brought her in crying and she often burst into tears shortly after they picked her up in the afternoon.

"You won't believe what happened Friday," Mary told them.

On her way out of school at the end of the day, a group of children surrounded Betsy, alternately woofing and calling her names. All she could do was sink to the floor. When her teacher walked into the hallway, the children scattered, leaving Betsy alone and sobbing.

"Oh, here's the cry-baby animal girl again" she muttered under her breath as she stood glaring down her nose at Betsy. "Get up and stop crying! This behavior has got to stop. I'm getting tired of your crying and your tantrums. You deserve a good walloping. If I were your parents . . ." the teacher started in on Betsy.

"You'd what?" interrupted Mary angrily. She had come to pick up Betsy from school and when she hadn't come out Mary had gone in to find her. She walked in to find Betsy in a heap on the floor with her teacher looming over her. It was all Mary could do to control herself. She was livid that this woman would treat her daughter this way. If there were only some way to make these people understand what Betsy was going through. She needed a way to make them realize that Tourette Syndrome was nothing that Betsy could control but that it didn't have to ruin her life. While Mary gathered Betsy up the teacher eyed them coolly. She clearly had no idea what the Verinis were facing.

Betsy's mother finds the teacher hovering over Betsy in the hallway.

"I am shocked to find such ignorant behavior in an educator," was all that Mary could trust herself to say before she left with her arm around Betsy.

After they had talked for about an hour Willie said, "So, if the doctor confirms that it's Tourette's we'll tell Betsy while we're there."

"I really do think that's the best because there already is such an incredible bond between them. Pepper has helped Betsy all along simply by being there. Perhaps there will come a time when Betsy will be able to help Pepper Belle," Bob replied.

The disorder they shared impacted the hopes and dreams of those who loved them. How they dealt with it would affect all their lives. They each wanted the best possible outcome for everyone.

Saturday arrived and, as usual, Betsy arrived a little early carrying the bag of carrots for Pepper. She was unusually quiet as they drove down the highway but grew more animated and less withdrawn as they grew closer. By the time they walked down the last corridor to the stalls, she was clearly happy with anticipation.

Pepper Belle had now been at Tufts for four weeks. During that time a video camera in her stall had been on recording her every move 24 hours a day. They had run numerous tests on her as well. Dr. Dodman had personally gone over all the results, all the assessments and much of the video. While Betsy visited Pepper Belle, he went over everything with Willie, Peggy and Big John. He told them that Pepper Belle had the symptoms of Tourette Syndrome and that he felt comfortable with that diagnosis. Since there was nothing more for them to do, they could bring her home the following Saturday.

Betsy was sitting on the hay, casually feeding Pepper carrots and talking quietly to her. The little radio was playing softly in the background. Pepper Belle was nuzzling Betsy gently and eating every carrot she was offered. When the Ferreros entered the stall, neither of them flinched.

Betsy tells Pepper that she has Tourette Syndrome, the same as Betsy.

"Betsy," Willie began, "Dr. Dodman has just given us his diagnosis of Pepper Belle and says she can come home next week."

Willie was hoping that if news of the diagnosis upset Betsy, knowing that Pepper would soon be home should make her happy and would get them past it. Betsy looked up at him expectantly.

"Dr. Dodman says that Pepper Belle has Tourette Syndrome, just like you." Willie said softly.

Betsy's eyebrows went up as her eyes opened wide. Her mouth didn't know what to do. It was caught between a frown and a smile. She didn't know what she felt. Her very best friend in the whole world had the same disorder that had made Betsy's world miserable. Betsy made a silent vow to do whatever she could to help make it easier on Pepper Belle. It was Betsy, with large tears slowly rolling down her cheeks, her arms around Pepper's neck and her face drawn close, who told Pepper Belle that she had Tourette Syndrome.

While the Ferreros were thinking about the practical aspects of bringing Pepper home, Pepper Belle's return was all Betsy could think or talk about both at home and at school. Her teacher was coldly polite when Betsy told her that Pepper Belle had the same medical condition that she had. The teacher continued to believe that there was no medical problem and that all Betsy really needed was the proper discipline. She was sure Betsy was making everything up about the horse and was getting annoyed by Betsy's story telling. If it weren't for her discussion with the principal after the incident in the hallway with Mary, she would have called Betsy a liar then and there. Mary had called the principal after she had heard the teacher mistreating Betsy. The principal's focus was the teacher's behavior, not Betsy's. The teacher did not relish another conversation like that.

Saturday couldn't arrive quickly enough for Betsy. They planned to leave around 9 AM and when Big John got up, he knew to expect her early. He was a bit startled however, when he got down to the barn around 6:30 AM to find Betsy already there and Pepper's stall decorated with red and pink hearts. He snickered to himself as he watched her preparing the stall with hay, and caught sight of the shoebox stuffed with carrots that she had brought with her. He helped her hang the "Welcome Home Pepper Belle" banner she had made with her mother. It was red, white and pink, decorated with hearts for Valentine's Day. He was tickled pink that she was so happy. As she walked around making sure that everything was set for Pepper's arrival, there was almost no sign that Betsy was any different from any other incredibly excited girl her age. Her focus and intensity made her forget the woofing and sleeve pulling.

Bob Verini had walked over to see if John and Willie needed a hand with anything. For a few minutes John and Bob stood by the barn door watching and listening to Betsy. She was working, buzzing back and forth laying new straw, washing the water pail and talking to Pepper at if she were actually there. Betsy, now almost 12 years old, seemed happy.

Betsy's father had a brass name-plate made for the stall door, "Pepper Belle" from your best friend "Betsy." When her father showed her what he had, she got even more excited. "John, John, see what I have," waving the shiny brass plate. "Can we put this on the door NOW?" John, good-naturedly, stopped his chores, got a screwdriver and mounted it on Pepper Belle's door. Betsy wiped the fingerprints off and bounced around like a chipmunk talking about Pepper.

It was now mid-February. The winter had been mild overall, but during the past few day the pattern had changed. On Friday morning they had gotten a couple of inches of snow, followed by a brief freezing rain shower. Since then it had remained overcast and just enough below freezing that nothing had melted. The trees, bushes, fences and roofs were covered with a light frosting of ice. The sun was beginning to break through the clouds and everything sparkled in the light. The whole place looked like a fairyland.

Pepper's decorated stall

Willie surveyed the scene from inside the house. He watched as Big John hitched the trailer to the truck with Betsy skipping excitedly around him. He had no idea what was in store for them in the future. Still, he felt good and was feeling positive about everything. John put Cool Pat and the other horses in the paddock and they set out. You couldn't shut Betsy down with a mouthful of peanut butter or bubble gum. As they approached Tufts she became more and more excited. They arrived about 10:30 AM.

When Betsy bounced out of the car she was carrying two bags. One bag was full of carrots but neither Willie nor John had any idea what might be in the other. Since they were picking Pepper Belle up to bring her home, they parked in a different place. Willie had pulled the truck into a parking lot next to a good size paddock.

Pepper Belle's handler was waiting by the gate and as soon as she saw Betsy she walked over to the truck. She spoke briefly to Big John and Willie and then took Betsy to see Pepper. When they arrived at Pepper's stall Betsy became very quiet and tears started down her cheeks. As the door opened, Betsy hugged Pepper around the neck. Pepper was very docile, as if she could understand the happiness of the moment.

Willie and John went to see Dr. Dodman. They waited a minute or two in his secretary's office and then Dr. Dodman welcomed them into his.

"I'd like to start her on some medication that should make it easier to handle the disorder. It will cost about $50 a day," Dr. Dodman said.

Big John and Willie looked at each other.

"No drugs for Pepper," Willie said emphatically. "Perhaps you don't understand," he said. "There are two reasons we won't be putting Pepper Belle on medication. First, the cost is quite prohibitive. $50 a day is simply outrageous and the drugs can't guarantee her well-being. Finally, Pepper Belle is a Standardbred race horse. We intend for her to race. Any type of drug would make her ineligible. It's illegal for a racehorse to use drugs."

Betsy hugs Pepper upon her release from Tufts.

"Surely the racing authority would understand that these drugs would not enhance her speed," Dr. Dodman began.

"There would be no exception," Willie said flatly.

Big John would continue to train Pepper Belle without the aid of medication. He told Dr. Dodman he would keep records of Pepper's training progress and of the progress of her disorder. He promised the doctor that if he learned anything he would pass it along. Willie and John assured the doctor that it was fine if he stopped by when he was in the area. He walked with them down to the paddock.

When Betsy saw Dr. Dodman, she ran over to the gate and picked up the bag she had been holding earlier. She raced back, pulled out a small framed picture and handed it to the doctor.

"I want you to have this so that you won't forget Pepper Belle," Betsy told Dr. Dodman in a tiny voice.

He looked at the picture she had given him. It was a picture of Pepper Belle giving Betsy a kiss. The doctor realized it must be a very special treasure to her. Thinking of the difficulties which lay ahead for each of them, he hoped that they would be able to continue to help each other. He thanked her for the picture and she gave him another big hug. Blinking back tears, he told Betsy he would do whatever he could to help Pepper Belle.

Now they were ready to say good-bye, Big John took out a brass and white leather lead shank which he had gotten for Pepper. A lead shank is something like a leash made specifically for horses. With the handler's assistance, Betsy fitted it over Pepper Belle and then led her out of the University's paddock for the trip home. When they got to the trailer, Big John had the door open and Pepper ran right into it.

"All right," called Willie. "Betsy, why don't you get into the truck while John gets everything set to roll?"

Betsy gives Dr. Dodman a picture of Pepper and her.

Betsy had other ideas. She had decided that she should ride in the trailer with Pepper Belle. Willie's immediate reaction was "NO!" Big John looked at his father and said, "Why not? I can ride with her!" Betsy calmly explained her reasons to Willie. Willie shook his head back and forth. Betsy looked up at Willie, tears forming slowly and simply said, "Please?"

All Willie could do was check the trailer to make sure that Big John had made it safe. He tucked them into the trailer and climbed into the truck for the drive home.

Betsy's parents joined Peggy waiting for Pepper Belle to return from Tufts. Peggy had prepared a Thanksgiving dinner in celebration of Pepper's return. She and Willie had invited Betsy's parents to join them. The excitement was thick as truck and trailer pulled into the yard.

Willie opened the trailer door and John backed Pepper Belle out. She was obviously pleased to be home. John gave the lead rope to Betsy. Under the "Welcome Home Pepper Belle" sign and into the heart covered stall they went. Pepper headed straight to the feed pail with carrots. John closed the stall door and as soon as Pepper finished her carrot treats, she frolicked, then rolled in the fresh bed of straw Betsy had made earlier.

Getting up, she shook from nose to tail as if to say, "Boy, is it good to be home." Betsy could hardly contain her happiness and hugged Pepper's neck repeatedly. Betsy's parents and Peggy came in the barn and everyone was in a festive mood. John knew something both Pepper and Betsy would like. He hitched Pepper up to the jog cart. Watching John, Betsy and Pepper jog around the track, it was clear that everyone was delighted that Pepper was home.

Betsy and John take Pepper Belle for a ride.

John and Betsy tucked Pepper into her stall and went into the house to join the feast. It was all there, right down to the cranberry sauce and pumpkin pie. Peggy said that it was a thanksgiving that Pepper Belle was home safe. The conversation centered on training Pepper to prepare her for a qualifying race. The radio blared out, "Moe" hit a home run for the Red Sox during a grapefruit league game in Tampa. Betsy sat quietly, beaming through the entire meal.

Although it was cold, little snow fell that winter and as March approached, John picked up training where they had left off prior to her trip to Tufts. Soon Pepper was jogging three to four miles a day. They were nearly always on the track when Betsy arrived after school. Pepper was a good student and learned well. The unpredictability of Tourette Syndrome sometimes made it difficult for John to train her. Betsy would talk quietly and soothingly to Pepper. When she sensed that John was getting frustrated, she would turn her attention and calming influence toward him.

Pepper enjoyed the daily routine, but at night she showed her Tourette's tics by kicking the walls and squeaking. John put kicking chains on Pepper's rear legs in an effort to slow down the kicking and reduce the chances of Pepper seriously hurting herself. Kicking chains are short chains, about eight inches, attached to a strap. When a horse kicks, these chains slap the side of the leg, discouraging the kicking. She also continued to spin around trying to bite her flanks. However, when Pepper was jogging, she showed no tics whatsoever.

Betsy came to see Pepper each day after school and all day Saturday and Sunday. The bond between the two grew deeper and it was obvious the two had a calming effect on each other. You could hear Betsy telling Pepper about how unhappy she was going to school and having to be with the kids that mocked her or completely stayed away from her. Sometimes she would become teary. Usually she just got very quiet for a few minutes.

Then she would jump up and brush Pepper whether she needed it or not.

It was the second week in May and the trees and flowers were showing signs of the birth of a new season. Soon robins started to appear trumpeting the arrival of spring. Trees budded and the grass showed signs of revival. In the morning when the horses were fed it was pleasant to listen to hundreds of birds in symphony. The tractors could be heard putting in the vegetable fields. In the neighboring Forbes Farm plants were being set out for the upcoming growing season. The days were quite hot and the nights were cool. Pepper Belle was about to grow into a race horse.

Pepper was advancing in her training to jogging five miles a day. She was going her training miles at a 2:35 clip. At this rate, it wouldn't be too long before Pepper would be ready to go to Plainridge Racetrack in Plainfield, Massachusetts and qualify to race. Young horses and horses that haven't run a race in more than a year, must first prove they can run in a qualifying race before they can take part in a betting race. A 2 year old must go a mile in 2:13 in order to qualify.

At various intervals, John would train Pepper with a special, heavier cart. This cart had a double seat. With the Verini's permission, and a safety helmet, he would let Betsy ride with him. Of course, this was most exciting to Betsy. She would have loved to share this feeling with her classmates but, as things were, she had to hold everything in.

The U.S. Trotting Association keeps records for all Standardbred race horses. The records begin with the horse's name, its parents, and the names of the owners. The Association then keeps information on each race a horse participates in, up to 40 races at a time. John had to register her name with the Association and then wait until he received Pepper Belle's "race papers" before he could enter her in a race.

Pepper Belle in springtime

As a result of their joint effort, Pepper had made amazing strides. She was physically fit and training well. She was a fine-tuned natural. While he waited for her papers, Big John felt Pepper was progressing to the point where she should be schooled behind "the starting gate." In order to begin a race, the horses must line up behind a gate attached to a moving car. When all the horses are lined up, the car speeds up and the gates fold up against the sides of the car like giant wings. Some horses had a difficult time with this and had trouble qualifying.

With all the other potential challenges facing Pepper, Big John wanted to be sure she would be comfortable going to the gate. He placed a ladder across the back of the truck. Willie drove the truck while John jogged Pepper along behind it. Betsy sat in the truck with Willie. She talked to Pepper through the open cab window in the back. John jogged Pepper up to the makeshift gate and she held the position a dozen or more times. John and Willie were satisfied that she showed no fear and were sure she'd have no trouble with the gate at Plainridge.

It was time to try Pepper behind a real gate. Training sessions were held at Plainridge each Saturday before the regular races. Betsy begged to go, so the entire Verini and Ferrero families decided to make a day of it.

The two families packed a lot of good food and drinks. John and Willie got the horse trailer and equipment ready. Saturday morning everyone met at the barn, the excitement in the air was obvious. Betsy bounded around bringing Pepper's water pail and of course, a bag full of carrots.

Pepper had learned to go in and out of the trailer since she was very young. John fed her grain in the trailer, parking it in the pasture with the loading ramp down. She never failed to load right on. Today was no different. She loaded on, the tailgate was closed, and off they went to Plainridge.

Betsy rode in the truck with Willie and John, while Peggy rode with Bob and Mary. They headed for the Mass. Pike. As they went through the last exit booth, Pepper started to act up to the point where John and Betsy got in the trailer and rode with Pepper a short few miles to the track. Willie guessed that maybe Pepper was having a tic of sorts but couldn't spin around because she was confined.

As they arrived at Plainridge, it was clear they were not going to the mall. In addition to the standard rows of cars you'd find in any parking lot, there was a diagonally parked row of trucks with horse trailers attached behind them. The trucks bore the names and colors of the different stables. It was a symphony of bright colors. Betsy was so excited she burst from the car when they arrived at the track. She could not contain her excitement.

The stables at the track were at once, similarly to and vastly different than the stable at home. The contents and the smells were basically the same but the similarity stopped there. Pepper's home at the Masconette Stable was a cozy barn with an abundance of flowers, kittens and cats. Here, there were many large barns and each might contain four to six different stables. John dropped everyone off and took Pepper to the paddocks. Peggy and Mary went to the grandstand. Willie and Betsy headed to the Office of the Racing Commissioner. Betsy would need a special pass that would allow her to go out into the barns and paddocks and onto the track. The track was a controlled, regulated environment. It was there for racing and people bet on races. Willie introduced Betsy to the people in the office and she was given her special pass. She clipped it to her sweater and was instantly free to go anywhere that Pepper went. Pepper Belle was in the paddocks and that was where Betsy wanted to be.

Drivers were on the track warming up horses and the sound of the horses trotting by was constant and comforting. Despite everyone's excitement, there was an underlying tension. How would Pepper Belle perform on the track? Would she go to the gate? How would she react to jogging on the big, open track with other horses?

Plainridge Racetrack

The paddock is a very busy barn area where horses are stabled during pre-race warm-ups, and waiting their turn to race. Each stall in the paddock has two numbers above it; indicating the race and the horse's position number at the starting gate. There were thirty horses going to qualify that day along with seven green horses to be schooled behind the starting gate. Everyone was buzzing around getting the horses ready and friends reviewed old acquaintances. The talk was of horses, racing, family, and friends. There were huddled conferences and good natured disagreements. The smell of straw was pungent. Everyone here had a badge indicating that they were there legally. Training and racing sulkies seemed to be strewn everywhere.

Danny Whitney, the driver of the starting gate and a good friend of Willie's, walked through the paddock. When he spotted Willie he went right over. Willie introduced Danny to everyone and after talking about various horses, Willie had an idea. Perhaps Betsy could get permission to ride with Danny in the Starter Car.

"Would you like that Betsy?" inquired Danny.

Betsy was taken aback at first and wasn't quite sure. Willie explained to her that it would be a lot like riding in the truck when they had used the ladder to practice. Betsy said "okay," but only if Willie was with her. Danny called the Judges and got permission for Willie and Betsy to ride in the Starter Car. They would ride during the four qualifying races in addition to the schooling. The next thing she knew, Betsy found herself walking out to the track with Willie to get into the Starter Car.

The Starter Car for a harness race is not at all like a car you would see on the street. Its roof, seating and wing-like gates set it apart. A large model car serves as the base. The roof of the car is removed and replaced with a low windowed box. It looked something like a convertible with a cereal box lying on its back sitting on top of it. The front seat of the car remained fairly standard. It was the rear seating area that was different. The standard back seat had been removed and replaced with what were more like two stools. Each one had a back that lay flat against the seat when no one was sitting in it. In order to sit down, you flipped the back up. These seats faced backwards toward the rear of the vehicle. The steel gate wings were pressed flat against the sides of the car. Although they were set high up so that the top of the gate was above the roof, they were fairly wide and came down lower than the top of a normal car. She had to duck low so that she wouldn't hit her head on the gate as she got in. The back of the seat was flipped up so that Betsy could slide onto it. She found herself sitting at a metal console. The "Starter" sat to Betsy's left. Set into the console in front of him was a speedometer and a lever.

Once Danny and Willie were settled in the front seat and the Starter was ready, the car rolled slowly around the track. When it was in position, the Starter used the lever to slowly unfold the gate wings. Once the gate was open, the car started to move slowly. The two folding gate arms were each about twenty feet long with the numbers 1—8 painted on them for the race horses to line up behind. The drivers pull the horses up behind the moving gate and line them up according to their starting position. The horses had to keep their noses right up to the gate in order to start a race. When every horse is in position, the Starter says "GO" and the starting gate arms close next to each side of the car and it speeds away to one side and the race is on.

Betsy did exactly what she was told but had a hard time keeping her composure. She was boiling over with excitement as she looked out the rectangular window. Willie sat in the front seat with Danny. Willie explained Tourette Syndrome to Danny and how Betsy and Pepper Belle were both affected.

The gate car leading horses.

After the thrill of starting the four qualifying races, the business of teaching young green horses was about to start. Peggy and the Verinis sat in the car parked at the rear side of the track. Pepper Belle, driven by John and six other horses, came on to the track and jogged around the 5/8 mile track three times to warm up. Then the starting gate opened its arms and started down the track. Pepper and the other horses came up behind the gate. Some of the horses were very reluctant, others reared up, two came right up. Pepper would have no part of it, and hung back. Pepper was accustomed to her track at home. She was not used to being sandwiched between other horses and their drivers. It was critical for her to be focused. John calmly talked to Pepper and tried to coax her along.

For such a long time Pepper Belle had been Betsy's focus. Pepper had always been there for Betsy. Today, Betsy knew she had an opportunity to be there for Pepper Belle and be her focus. Betsy was allowed to talk because this wasn't a real race. She started yelling, "Come on Pepper, come on Pepper!" Pepper perked her ears forward and realized her buddy was in this big monster in front of her. Betsy kept on calling. Now, three of the seven horses were right up to the gate, one had gone back to the Paddock. Pepper was furthest back but had started to come closer. Either she was not assured that the monster wasn't going to bite her or she could see Betsy calling, but Pepper did make it to the gate with the other five horses and circled the track three times. The Starter then went faster and pulled away as if to start a race. All of a sudden, six horses were racing for the first time, although slowly. Three of the other horses broke. Even though Pepper came in next to last, she never broke.

The driver let Betsy and Willie off at the paddock. Betsy flew up to her mother and father like a cannon ball. She couldn't stop telling everyone how great it was. Then all of a sudden her attention went to Pepper. Big John had taken Pepper to the wash stall and was hosing her down. Then he covered her with a cooler.

Pepper was very tired. After all, this was the biggest workout she had ever had.

Driving home Peggy had suggested stopping at the State Park which was right on the way. Everyone agreed. Willie parked the trailer rig in the shade while the Verinis parked close to the picnic tables. John gave Pepper hay and left the trailer doors open. The food was spread out on the picnic table. Everyone had an appetite, and the food disappeared as they laughed and talked about the day's events. One odd pigeon and a couple of squirrels begged for food. Betsy threw some cookies to the squirrels. Big John chased one of the squirrels up a tree and made Betsy laugh. Pepper started stamping her feet to let everyone know she wanted to go home.

When the caravan arrived home, Betsy was allowed to put Pepper in the straw bedded stall. She immediately rolled over and over, as horses do, shook herself and started eating her grain. Big John shut the barn lights off and bid everyone good night. Arnie, the big Shepherd, followed John to the house. Betsy came over on Sunday after church and spent a couple of hours in the "bush" pasture with Pepper. You could see Betsy smack the horse flies as they dared to land on Pepper Belle.

Betsy had two and a half weeks left of school before summer vacation. The teacher was planning some fun activities to end the year. A class picnic was being planned at Forest Park in Springfield, Massachusetts. Everyone was excited except Betsy. She feared being in a free atmosphere with all the kids. Although it seemed that Betsy's tics had become less frequent, the kids still enjoyed tormenting her, all of them except for Jason. Jason was a year older than most of the kids in the class. He had to repeat a year due to a long illness. Jason didn't join in when the kids called Betsy "Woof Girl." When they tormented her, he told her not to pay attention to them.

This was a crack in the hostile wall she faced every day. Usually Betsy ate her lunch in the classroom rather than the lunchroom with everyone else. One day Jason opened the door and sheepishly asked Betsy if she would like some company. Very quietly, Betsy said "Yes, please come in." Not much was said as they finished lunch. Jason mentioned the picnic and wondered if Betsy was going. "No, I don't want to go" was Betsy's immediate reply. Jason wanted to try to persuade her but somehow knew there was no point in it. When Betsy got home that day she made her usual express trip to the barn to see her pal Pepper.

Betsy talking to Pepper was a daily occurrence. It had gotten so that Big John didn't pay much attention. Today he overheard her telling Pepper about a "friend." This got Big John's attention. Betsy told Pepper about lunch with Jason and how nice he was to her. She told Pepper she wasn't going to the picnic.

Big John told Betsy's mother what he had heard. She couldn't hold back a smile. Betsy being accepted by anyone had all but disappeared with the onset of Tourette's. Betsy went to school those last days with a little more willingness. She told Jason all about Pepper Belle. Jason shared her excitement; he had experience with horses because he had lived on a dude ranch in New Hampshire before moving to East Longmeadow. His job was to clean stalls and groom horses. In the afternoons, he had gone riding with his buddy, Mike Call.

Betsy told him about how Pepper Belle was training to enter a race. She told him that John had said she could go if it was on a Saturday. When school was out, she would be allowed to go any day. A funny thing happened. Since Jason had started talking to Betsy, a lot of the other kids began to leave her alone. This made life a little easier. Still, the class picnic came and went. True to her word, Betsy did not go.

The next, and last, social event before school let out was a visit by the singing group, "The Coasters," in the school auditorium with the other classes. The group was in the area to do a benefit concert. In order to generate a little excitement for that, they had volunteered to perform at the high school. The kids were allowed to invite their parents and friends. Betsy's mother, Peggy and Willie attended. The auditorium was jammed full.

Jason and Betsy talking

The Coasters often ask for volunteers from the audience to go on stage to participate in some of their antics. If no one volunteers, or if there are too many, they head into the audience to grab "volunteers" themselves and literally pull them up to the stage. Betsy's class was seated in the front row and they grabbed Betsy's hand. The situation caused her to "woof" loudly and some of her classmates couldn't resist yelling out "Woof Girl." Betsy was so embarrassed, she broke away and ran out the door. When her mother and Willie caught up to her, she was sobbing loudly, hands over her face, trying to cover the tears that were streaming down her cheeks. Would it never end? Only four days remained of the school year, but Betsy did not go. She would not face the embarrassment.

On the 4th of July, the town of East Longmeadow always had a huge parade. It was the largest parade in the state. Following the parade, Willie and Peggy always hosted a big barbecue. This year was no exception. This year the Ferreros had a lot to celebrate. John jogged Pepper around the track and people lined the fence to cheer her on.

John was satisfied with the way things had gone with the gate at Plainridge and with the way Pepper's training was going. Pepper trained extremely well the next week and had a time of 2:15. Qualifying races were held on Thursdays at Plainridge Raceway. The first Thursday after the 4th of July, Willie, Peggy, John, Betsy and her mom set off to the track to watch Pepper's attempt to qualify. John didn't really expect that she would qualify her first time out. John entered Pepper to race and drew the infamous 8th hole on the starting gate in the first race. Bob had to work so Betsy, Mary and Peggy rode down in the Chevy Super Cab truck with Willie and John.

The excitement, worry and anticipation grew as post time neared. John and Willie's good friend, Ralph Anderson, was put on as driver. Ralph was gentle with young horses and treated Pepper like a lady. He took her around the track twice before the race to warm her up and gave Pepper a chance to know she had a new driver. There were five qualifiers that day. The fifth race had only four horses instead of the usual eight.

The paddock judge soon announced, "Line 'em up for the first race." Driver Ralph Anderson took the reins and John led Pepper out of the paddock. Everything seemed fine. Betsy stood on the rail next to the paddock with Willie. Peggy and Mary were sitting in the grandstand. Everyone was quiet except for Betsy's low whisper, "Do it Pepper, you can do it." Ralph took two warm-up laps with the other horses and then the Starter called the horses to the gate.

The gate started at a low speed, allowing the horses to come up to their mark on the gate. One by one, each of the horses took its place, that is except one, Pepper Belle. She would not go near it. The starting gate proceeded and the race started. Pepper was about twenty lengths behind the gate at the start and then, to add insult to injury, she broke. She would be disqualified. Everyone was disappointed. Betsy had tears in her eyes as Pepper came off the track. Pepper showed no signs of being tired, after all, she had only jogged around the track.

The judge called to confirm that Pepper had been disqualified. This meant another week wasted unless Willie asked the judge for something that is usually never done. He wanted to let Pepper try again in the fifth race today. Willie explained the circumstances to the judge. He wanted the judge to let Pepper Belle run in the eighth race and to let Betsy ride with the race Starter. The judge told Willie it was not possible. Willie, not wanting to take no for an answer, persisted. The racing industry had never dealt with a horse with Tourette Syndrome and he thought maybe a concession would be in order. The judge hesitated a moment and then decided that Willie had made his case. As there were only four horses in the fifth race, Pepper would fit in the 5th hole. The judge said, "Go ahead, I'll deal with the paperwork."

Willie hustled over to Pepper's stall yelling to John, "Get her ready for the fifth race!" John couldn't believe what he had just heard. As he put the harness back on, Willie took Betsy to the starting gate. The judge had radioed to Danny, the driver, that it would be fine for Betsy to ride in the Starter Car. It was easy for Betsy to go this time, for she already knew the Driver and Starter from the schooling session a couple of weeks ago. Horses from the third race were just coming out of the paddock as Betsy piled in. The thrill Betsy experienced and the wide-eyed happy look was almost indescribable. Willie had told Betsy to call to Pepper when she was warming up before the race to let Pepper know that Betsy was in the car. Betsy sat with the Starter during the third and fourth races, talking about her best friend, Pepper Belle. The Starter knew both Betsy and Pepper Belle had Tourette Syndrome. He was friendly and understanding and tried to ignore Betsy's woofing and incessant sleeve pulling.

It was not long before the horses for the fifth race came out of the paddock and there, sporting Number 5, was Pepper. The horses have to pass right by the starting gate to take their warm-up lap. Betsy called out, "Pepper, Pepper!" Pepper's ears went up in recognition.

Ralph Anderson and Pepper Belle took the warm-up lap and the starting gate started to move. The Starter allowed Betsy to call Pepper. The first few horses were in place. This time, Pepper was only a short distance off and coming. When the gate reached the starting pole, Pepper's nose was almost touching the gate.

"GO!" The race was on. The first time around, Pepper was 5th and remained there until the beginning of the long Plainridge finish stretch. She passed one, two, then three horses and as the finish line flashed past, Pepper had finished 2nd in 2:09. Betsy hugged the Starter and with tears of joy in her eyes kept repeating, "She did it. She did it!"

Back at the paddock, Big John and Willie were literally jumping. It must have been contagious because everyone in the paddock was cheering for Pepper. The horses came off the track. This time Pepper was sweaty and blowing a little. That didn't stop Betsy from planting a big kiss right on the end of Pepper's nose. Big John took over and shortly everyone was back in the truck headed home. Ralph had told Willie and John that during the race Pepper showed no signs of any Tourette's tics and was easy to handle. What a day! Everyone was exhausted and happy. Betsy fell asleep on the way home.

John decided that Pepper Belle would get two weeks rest and then enter her first actual race. Betsy went to the barn every day. She was determined to do everything she could to help Pepper Belle. The Big Day was drawing near and Pepper was to have her first real race Saturday at Plainridge Raceway. By now, usual preparations were made and the Verini and Ferrero families all piled into their vehicles.

Betsy rode with Big John and Willie. "Will I be able to go into the paddock with you?" asked Betsy. The judges didn't usually allow kids or unlicensed people in the paddock during Pari-Mutuel races, so Willie told her she would have to sit in the grandstand with her family and Peggy. Pepper drew the number 1 hole in the ninth race. When they arrived at Plainridge, John and Willie took Pepper Belle and the equipment into the paddock. Betsy hugged Pepper and told her, "Now, you be good." Then they all left for the grandstand. Popcorn and lemonade were the order for the day for the folks in the grandstand. That, plus a long wait for the ninth race.

In the paddock, Big John cross tied Pepper in her stall. Willie stayed with Pepper while John went to get a hamburger in the paddock kitchen. It was a warm, sunny day and everything seemed perfectly normal. When John got back, he started to put the bridle on Pepper. She went crazy, rearing up, kicking the stall walls, squeaking and generally acting upset and mean. You don't want a horse acting like this before a race because they use up the energy they will need in the race. The squeaking drew a lot of attention from the other horsemen. Everyone tried to help but things got worse. Willie turned to John and said, "Do you think that just maybe the trouble is that Betsy isn't here?"

Betsy calming down Pepper.

Just about then, Mr. Piontkowski, the owner of Plainridge, came over to see what was going on. Mr. Piontkowski was a very understanding person. He had owned race horses before and had gotten to know Willie. After an explanation of Pepper's behavior, Willie mentioned about Betsy's calming effect on Pepper. Perhaps Mr. Piontkowski could persuade the judges to give Betsy special permission to come into the paddock. Mr. Piontkowski didn't know if he could persuade the judges but would go up and talk to them. If anyone could get the job done, it was Mr. Piontkowski. Willie kept his fingers crossed as they waited for a call on the loud speaker. Sure enough, about fifteen minutes later it came. "Willie Ferrero, come to the paddock judges office." Willie left and yelled to John, "I hope it's the right message." It was. She could come to the paddock. The judge told Willie he could take a golf cart and go out to get her in order to save time. In no time Betsy was in the paddock sporting a special "race day" badge.

As long as John didn't try to harness Pepper, she stood still. Betsy found Pepper standing still. She went up to her as she did at home, speaking softly and calmingly to her.

Everyone nearby watched as John again started to harness her. Betsy's presence was like magic. Before you knew it, she was all harnessed and hitched to the jog cart going to the track. Betsy walked along side of her and sat on the rail. Pepper went out on the track with John for her first warm-up. Ralph Anderson came over after a couple of races and took Pepper out for her second warm-up. She gave a little trouble going on the track at first but John and Ralph talked her through it, and away she went. When they came back, Ralph said she was a little gimpy but behaved like a lady. When they finally called for the ninth race, Pepper led the eight horses to the track.

When the Starter called the horses, Pepper started shaking her head and giving Ralph a real hard time. When she went by the paddock gate, Betsy and Big John were yelling to Pepper, trying to reassure her. She mellowed out a little and Ralph got her rolling toward the gate. When the Starter said "GO," she was already a length off. By the time she reached the 1/4 mile pole she was in 8th place. Everyone was deflated. Going around the last turn she was still eighth. Ralph pulled her out, she passed the seventh, sixth, and fifth horses and finished fifth.

Pepper had done fairly well, earning her first money (5% of $1500), even though she did look gimpy. When Ralph brought her back, Betsy came out and she and Big John took off for the wash stalls. Ralph told Willie what he thought should be done from a driver's point of view. Ralph said she seemed a little sore making her rough in the turns but she paid attention to business all through the race.

Standardbred horses usually race about once each week. Because Pepper was a little sore, John decided to skip a week and work on her legs. Big John surmised the trouble was being caused by Pepper's wall kicking. Although the kicking chains helped a lot, John decided to nail some athletic floor pads to Pepper's walls. When she did kick it would soften the impact. Each day Pepper's legs were watered down for half an hour to make sure the heat was out. Betsy would hold the hose, chase horse flies and talk. Arnie would lie in the shade near by and watch like a mother hen.

Arnie was very protective of people. Any quick movement by any horse would cause Arnie to get in between the person and the horse. If a small child wandered in the direction of the horses, he would get in front of the child and push him or her back with his nose. One morning Peggy and her dear friend Ethel came to see the horses in the paddock. When someone came to the paddock the horses would come running up to the fence looking for carrots. Arnie took this as a threatening gesture. He would immediately run into the paddock barking and running to and fro to keep the horses away. Ethel and Peggy finally convinced Arnie it was okay and fed Cool Pat and the other horses some carrots.

When it came time for Pepper to race again, she was starting to look exceptional. Big John entered her and she drew the 4th hole in the eleventh and last race of the day on Friday. It was two weeks since Pepper's last race. John had trained her a little extra on Monday and she showed no signs of being sore.

It now became a ritual that when Pepper raced, all the Verinis and Ferreros raced also. This time, when they arrived at Plainridge Raceway, Betsy sported her special ID badge and was allowed to go in the paddock with Willie and Big John. Pepper was real feisty going in and John had to take a good hold of her. Betsy had a small stool and sat in the stall with Pepper. This time when John started to harness her, Pepper was still feisty but no trouble. She went out and warmed up with Big John and then Ralph without incident. When John went past the grandstand, Peggy and the Verinis were waving and cheering from the sidelines.

Finally it was time. The paddock judge called for the horses to line up for the eleventh race. Every horse being accounted for, the order to go to the track was given. "Take 'em out!" the judge yelled.

As Pepper went out, Betsy sat on the paddock fence and called to her. The warm-up laps went without incident. The starting gate moved slowly as the horses fell into their positions. In the 4th hole, Pepper had horses on either side of her for the first time. This seemed to do her good. When the Starter said "GO" she was passed on the outside, putting her in sixth place. Ralph decided to follow the two outside horses. At the stretch Pepper was still sixth but now starting to gain on the other horses on the inside. The announcer yelled, "Pepper Belle is making a move." After two more calls the announcer excitedly yelled, "Pepper Belle is nose to nose with Liberty Girl, the leading horse." Pepper pulled away two lengths and won the race. Betsy, John and Willie were sky high with excitement. Plainridge provides a golf cart for those in the paddock wishing to go to the winner's circle. Willie drove and John hung onto Betsy. The Verinis and Peggy were already there. Everyone gathered around to be photographed. Pepper Belle bent her head down and Betsy was hugging and talking to her as tears of happiness streamed down her cheeks.

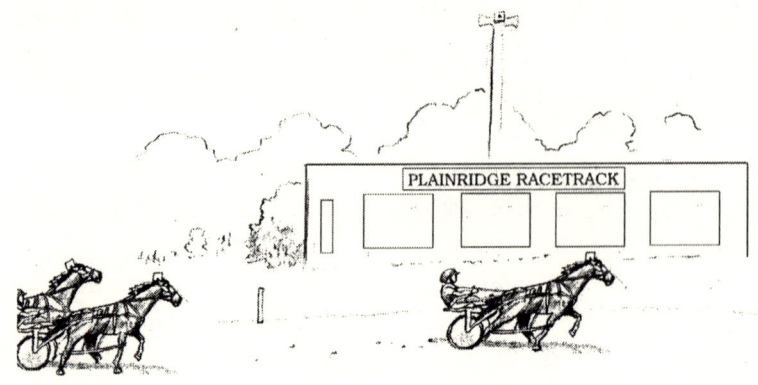

Pepper Belle pulls away for the win!

The picture was taken and Pepper Belle, led by John, started walking back toward the paddock. Ralph rode in the golf cart with Willie and Betsy. Betsy was on an emotional high. What a difference from the Betsy that had run out of the auditorium door just a few weeks ago. Pepper had truly lifted Betsy out of depression and gave her a wonderful reason to wake up each day.

Life at the farm changed a little now that they had a winner in the barn. Willie told everyone that even though Pepper had Tourette Syndrome she could still be a winner. Betsy would listen and a smile would creep over her face. Since school was out, Betsy walked down the dewy grass covered road to the horse barn every morning. A routine was set up for Betsy when she came over each morning. Her chores included picking up Pepper's stall, washing and filling the water pail, and sweeping out the barn. The best part was that Betsy got to take Pepper out on a lead rope and let her eat grass out in front of the homestead like she had done when she was a foal.

Betsy would watch the bluebirds flit about, collecting food for their babies in the birdhouse. A squirrel with white ears always came around. He was accustomed to getting crackers from Peggy and Willie and so he would come to beg. The squirrel would keep one eye on Arnie and one on Betsy. As soon as a cracker was thrown, he would pick it up and scamper up a tree to his eating branch. If the squirrel happened to run by Pepper, she would pick up her tail and prance around like a young flirting filly, to the delight of Betsy. Because Pepper was only two years old, Big John wanted two weeks before racing again, and race she did! After getting the 1st hole she fell back to the 6th and then put on a show. She passed everyone, including the big favorite, and won by four lengths. The announcer yelled that she had won her second race in a row and that Ralph Anderson never took the whip off his shoulder. It didn't take long before the regulars at Plainridge knew all about Pepper Belle and her mascot, Betsy. They quickly became the "darlings" of Plainridge. A picture taken by the track photographer of Pepper and Betsy appeared in one of the Plainridge programs and was captioned "A Winning Team!" Betsy was thrilled beyond words.

Pepper had a few more things to pull though. Up to this point, Pepper was really easy to load on the trailer. Suddenly, after her second win, she could not be loaded. Finally, a group of horsemen got together and forced her in. Sometimes people with Tourette Syndrome developed problems about going through doors. Now the star horse had developed the same thing. Willie solved this problem by installing a winch in the trailer. A safety halter was put on Pepper and she was pulled on board.

Each race the rest of the season was an adventure. Pepper raced fourteen times during the summer and fall. She compiled a wonderful record of four wins, four second places and two thirds. Betsy and Pepper still had their tics, but never when Pepper raced or Betsy was busy working on her chores. It seemed that when either of them was deeply involved and focused, the tics were minimal or nonexistent.

When Betsy went back to school in the fall, Jason was again in her class. At least Betsy would have one person to talk to about her breathtaking summer. Jason listened and was really impressed when Betsy showed him the picture that had appeared in the program. Some of the other kids overheard the tales of the summer adventure. When they saw the picture they began chiming in with questions. They found themselves talking to Betsy, enthused over all the wins Pepper Belle had had. Perhaps some of the kids were beginning to understand that Tourette Syndrome was not the end of the world and that you could still be a winner. Betsy's marks shot up as she was accepted by more of the other kids.

The Darlings of Plainridge

A winning team!

Pepper wins again!

Time flew by, early fall blew into early winter, the sky was often gray and overcast. The trees looked like skeletons against the sky. Just before Christmas snow fell and they were treated to a joyous white Christmas. Then it was New Year's and Pepper's two month rest came to an end.

Betsy went back to school after Christmas break. Even though her tics showed up once in a while, most of the kids came to understand that there was nothing she could do about it. She started to participate in class functions and, in general, her school life was improved. She was thankful for Pepper and Jason.

Big John plowed the snow off the track and jogged Pepper three miles a day. John was in no hurry as the track didn't re-open until the end of May. Betsy came over each day after school and did her chores. On Saturday and Sunday John would take her on the two-person sulky, teaching her how to drive. Betsy was growing up and it wouldn't be too long before she would be able to jog Pepper all by herself.

As time passed, Pepper was training a few faster miles. Spring was once again around the corner. The crocuses poked their heads out of the mulch next to the south side of the barn. Betsy saw the first robin on her way over one morning. When the track opened, Big John had Pepper motoring quickly and announced it was time to race.

Pepper Belle drew the 1st hole in the first race the following Saturday. All the excitement that had been dormant since Pepper's last race took new life. The hectic pace of getting ready was back. Pepper was in good shape, her coat was shining and her feisty attitude was boiling.

Betsy learning to drive the cart

Willie, Big John and Betsy got their new paddock badges and everything was in place. When the Verini and Ferrero entourage arrived, they all helped bring the equipment and Pepper into the race paddock. When the paddock judge closed the paddock gates to the public, everyone without badges had to leave. Peggy and the Verinis went to the grandstand rail to watch as Big John warmed up Pepper Belle. Peggy remarked how it was a thrill to see her son and Pepper out on the track.

After the first warm-up, Betsy got fresh water and brushed Pepper to a shine. Ralph Anderson soon came in greeting everyone, especially Betsy. Ralph took Pepper out for her second warm-up and came back with a big smile and exclaimed, "Boy, is she hot to go." There were four seasoned horses with outstanding track records in the race with her. Pepper would have her hands full today.

After about an hour, the paddock judge called the horses for the first race. Betsy walked along side of Pepper as she pranced out to the track. The crowd remembered Pepper Belle and Betsy. The announcer called, "They're back again!" As Pepper passed the clubhouse and the grandstand a cheer went up from the small crowd. Small kids, big kids, young and old kids all were calling, "Pepper, Pepper." Willie, Betsy and Big John were watching excitedly on the closed circuit TV monitor. Happy tears on Betsy's cheeks moved everyone in the paddock. It was a moment to remember.

The Starter called the horses to the gate and started to move down the straightaway. Eight horses got in position with no incident and in a moment the race was on. The two big favorites went to the front while Pepper Belle held on to the third position. At the 5/8 pole, two horses behind Pepper pulled out and passed Pepper on the outside. The third horse was next to Pepper and had boxed her in on the rail. As the horses approached the middle of the last turn, the horse boxing in Pepper on the rail pulled ahead. Ralph immediately went three wide and in a flash Pepper Belle was challenging the lead horse. A few more steps and she was a length ahead and looked like a sure winner again. The people in the grandstand were yelling and everyone was excited that their favorite was in the lead.

Then, all of a sudden, it happened. Pepper Belle looked like she stumbled and barely caught herself from going down. Ralph pulled her up, as all the other horses went by the finish. Pepper was standing in front of the grandstand, about one hundred feet from the finish line, unable to take a step. The winning horse had its picture taken but there seemed to be no cheering. In fact, there was a hush throughout the raceway. Ralph was holding Pepper by her head and watched as she tried to put her right foot down. She couldn't put any weight on it. She couldn't walk. Willie, Big John, Betsy and the track veterinarian arrived quickly on the golf cart. The vet started to examine her leg as Betsy tried to hold back her tears. Pepper Belle was all sweaty. You could see the expanded veins in her pumping nostrils, the result of her giant effort to win. A few of the young children were calling to Pepper softly. The vet summoned the track horse trailer as there was no way Pepper would be walking back to the paddock. The tailgate was let down. Big John, the vet and many horsemen who had jumped the rail to help, got Pepper Belle in the trailer. Big John, Pepper and Betsy rode back to the paddock together. Betsy was holding the lead rope and trying to comfort Pepper. As the trailer left for the paddock, everyone cheered and called to Pepper as she went by. It would be the last time Pepper would hear a cheering race track crowd. When they got back to the paddock, the vet told Willie and John that Pepper had blown a tendon and possibly broken a sesamoid bone as well. The X-ray he ordered showed the sesamoid bone with a hairline crack and the tendon ruptured from top to bottom.

The track vet examines Pepper.

Pepper was given a shot to relieve the pain and was given emergency treatment at the track. Betsy began woofing as the vehicles pulled onto the Ferreros' property. She stayed in the stall with the crippled Pepper and soon was calm and quiet again.

John called Dr. O'Leary and explained what had happened. The doctor arrived in about a half hour. He gave Pepper another shot for pain and then he and John put a cast on her foot. They would have to let the tendon cool out before wrapping it. It was near midnight before Dr. O'Leary went home. He was great with horses and both Willie and Big John were thankful that he was nearby and could come over so late. The doctor had also spent some time assuring Betsy that with a little time Pepper would be okay. When she was comfortable with that, she went home with her family, exhausted. On the way into the house, Willie remarked that Pepper had come a long way since that night when she was foaled. Those were fond memories and the thought brought a few chuckles to Big John.

The months to come during the summer meant lots of work for John. Betsy was a big help and was like a shadow to John, and Arnie was like a shadow to Betsy. The three of them were practically inseparable. It was a real hot August and the horse flies seemed over plentiful. August was memorable not because of the heat or the flies but because Pepper was now walking outside the barn and eating grass in front of the homestead with Betsy and Arnie in attendance. Between Pepper's tail and Betsy, the flies didn't stand a chance.

Betsy was rather unhappy when she had to go on vacation the last two weeks of August with her parents. She would only have a week afterward to be with her horse. Predictably, Betsy's first place to go when she got home from vacation was to see her buddy, Pepper. If Pepper had been a dog, she would have jumped in Betsy's lap. It was hard to tell which one was the happiest.

Arnie, Betsy and John

The question facing the Ferreros was what to do with Pepper Belle. Her racing days were over. Maybe a carriage horse, a brood mare, or what? Soon a decision would have to be made.

The week ended. September put a chill in the night air and a few colored leaves began to show up. It was the start of the school season. Betsy went to school and most of the same kids were in her class. Several of them told Betsy they had seen the article in the paper announcing the end of Pepper Belle's racing career. Betsy's school life continued to be pretty good even though she still had her tics and, at times, could not stop tugging on her sleeve. Her new teacher was wonderful. She did not scold Betsy for things she had no control over. She also was very strict about harassing behavior. Betsy felt more comfortable than she had in years.

Willie continued to ponder what to do with Pepper Belle. He and Peggy were talking about Betsy when the kernels of an idea began to form. Betsy was having a better time in school because the other kids had learned something about Tourette Syndrome through information about Pepper Belle. Perhaps Pepper could be used as a means of educating others about Tourette Syndrome. Maybe they could take Pepper to schools. It could help other children with Tourette Syndrome if there was a better understanding of the disorder. Peggy agreed wholeheartedly and challenged Willie with questions about how this could be done. That was all that he needed, a challenge.

If he was going to bring Pepper to school to educate others about Tourette Syndrome, he would have to learn more about it himself and have information to pass out in schools. He figured the first thing he should do would be to contact a Tourette Syndrome organization and ask for help. On Monday morning Willie sat at his desk and tried to find a telephone number in the directory. There was nothing listed. He called Directory Assistance. The operator told him there was no listing. Peggy suggested that he call the United Way. The head of the Greater Springfield United Way told him that he had never heard of any organization for Tourette Syndrome. Willie couldn't believe what he was hearing, but would not give up. The family doctor knew of no organization. He suggested that Willie call the local hospitals. The hospital managers couldn't help him.

Willie had spent an afternoon on the phone and gotten nowhere. He walked out to talk to Big John. John was just bringing Rain Rein Reign in from a training mile. He was preparing him for a race Friday at Yonkers Raceway. Big John had no suggestions, so the search was put on the back burner for now.

Willie frequently had a hard time falling asleep at night. Peggy didn't like the radio, so Willie had installed an ear speaker attached to the radio so he could listen and get relaxed without bothering her.

That Monday night Willie couldn't sleep and had the ear speaker in his ear. At precisely 3 AM a Buffalo, New York station announced time and call letters. Willie had never heard of this station before. He was amazed he was receiving a station so far away. The next words were:

"Anyone interested in contacting the National Tourette Syndrome Association, please call," and then they gave the number. Instinctively, he grabbed a pencil on the night stand and wrote down all but one number from memory. "This is odd," Willie thought. "How could this happen tonight when this afternoon no one could give me this number?" It seemed to him that a significant third party had something to do with it. Coincidence just didn't explain it.

The next morning Willie went to work at the process of elimination to determine the number he couldn't remember. The call went through to the National Tourette Syndrome Association in Bayside, New York. Willie was connected to Sue Levi-Pearl, Director of Scientific and Medical Programs, who listened to Willie's tale on how he got the number. She then asked Willie what she could do for him. "Nothing," he replied. "I was thinking I might be able to do something for you."

Willie writes down the phone number for the National Tourette Syndrome Association.

He explained how he owned a harness horse that had been diagnosed with a Tourette Syndrome-like affliction. He told her about Dr. Dodman at Tufts. The horse was named Pepper Belle. Willie briefly sketched the story of Pepper Belle and Betsy. He explained how he thought the horse had helped Betsy by showing the kids in her school that even though she had Tourette Syndrome, she was a winner.

As usual, Willie was brimming with ideas about what he could do. One idea was to have a "Pepper Belle Day" at Plainridge Raceway where a specially named race for Pepper Belle would be the feature. They could have a huge track-side barbecue and invite people with Tourette's all along the east coast to attend. The news media would certainly go for a horse-kid story and many people would benefit by the coverage. Perhaps Pepper could tour some schools. Sue listened without speaking and then told Willie that she would have Mark Levine from the national office return his call.

Willie didn't know what to expect. Had he spoken too much, too quickly, too loudly or what? He sat at his desk in silence hoping he had done the right thing. Then he went out to the barn. Big John was cleaning the harness and getting ready for the race at Yonkers when Willie told him what had just transpired. At the same time, Betsy came in to take Pepper for her daily grassing. Rain Rein Reign was bouncing around the stall and rearing up on his hind legs letting everyone know he was ready to race.

Wednesday morning Mark Levine called. After they introduced themselves to each other Mark said, "Sue called a management staff meeting after speaking to you yesterday. She said she wasn't absolutely sure you were for real but that you gave her more ideas in five minutes than we have had in five years."

Mark told Willie that the study being conducted at Tufts was sponsored by the Tourette Syndrome Association and that he had already spoken to Dr. Dodman and confirmed Willie's story. Credibility was established. Mark had been asked to arrange a meeting with Willie as soon as possible. Willie suggested they meet at Yonkers Raceway on the coming Friday. A location at the harness gate was agreed to.

That Friday was a memorable night. Trailers were arriving carrying the horses for the evening's races. Horses going to race are known to act up a bit. When a big gray trotter started backing towards Mark, he quickly retreated behind Willie. Of course, he wasn't scared, he was just being polite and letting Willie go first.

A visit to the judges' office got Mark a special pass to enter the paddock area and sit in the owners' and trainers' glassed in stand. Rain Rein Reign was in the seventh race. Big John was doing all the work getting him ready for the race giving Mark and Willie plenty of time to talk. Mark said that one of the things he wished to accomplish that night was to get Willie's permission to use Pepper Belle's name in the future. Many subjects were discussed and the night ended with what might be called a win-win situation.

Rain Rein Reign won the race. An understanding that Pepper Belle would be the official mascot of the Tourette Syndrome Association was agreed to. They would develop a program for the advancement of awareness of Tourette Syndrome using Pepper.

Even though it was raining going home, the trip seemed very short. Rain Rein Reign's First Place share of the purse brought in some much needed farm money. Finally, Pepper Belle's future seemed to be revealing itself.

Willie was very friendly with Fred, the local school superintendent, and made it a point to sit with him at the next Rotary meeting. Fred knew of other kids in the school system with Tourette's. He told Willie the idea of bringing Pepper Belle to school sounded "do-able." Mark Levine and Dr. Dodman were each asked if they would like to participate. A date was set with the principal of the East Longmeadow High School and the program was put together.

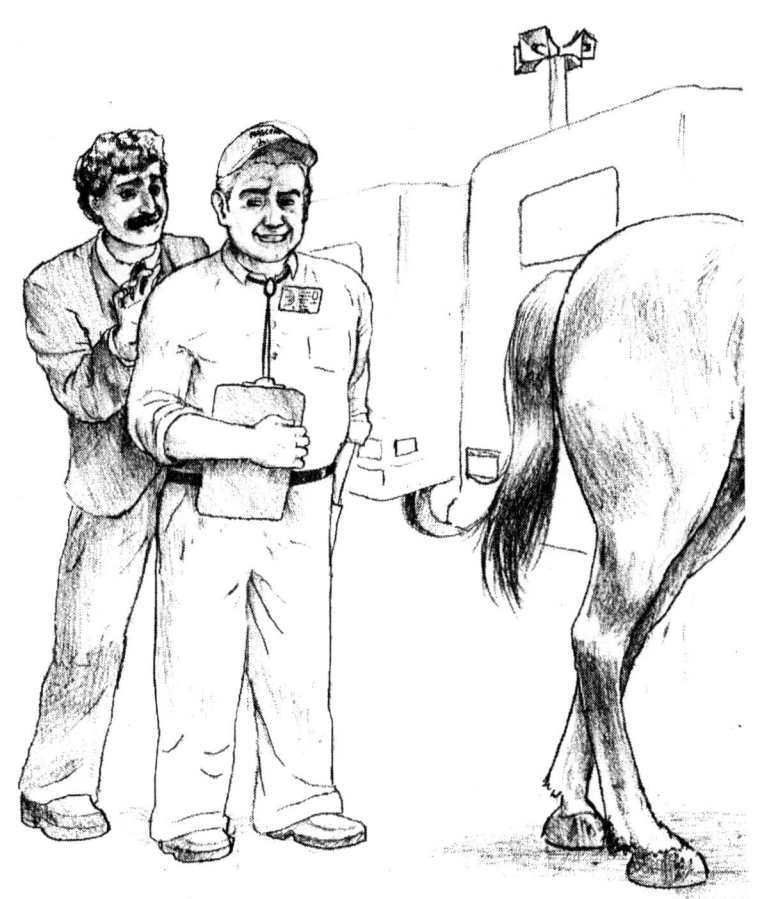

Willie with Mark Levine at Yonkers Raceway

Big John brought Pepper to the high school front lawn. The students from the ninth grade watched here as she paraded around with John. Then they were allowed to gather round Pepper Belle, touch her and ask questions. It was a good experience. Most of the kids had never been around a horse before. The program then continued in the auditorium. Mark Levine opened with a short discussion of Tourette Syndrome. The students then watched a clip from the Maury Povitch Show. It showed several children and the way their tics affected them. The audience was touched. Dr. Dodman followed with an explanation of the parallel disease in animals. He showed films of Pepper from her stay at Tufts. She bit her flanks, kicked out at the padded walls and squeaked. Now, everyone was seeing Pepper Belle at her worst.

Willie then showed a video of Pepper at her best. They watched her racing and winning at Plainridge Raceway. The response was positive. One of the students said that it was incredible seeing the horse outside, watching the Tufts video and then seeing the video of Pepper Belle race and win. That it was the same horse was amazing.

Mark closed out the program by inviting the students to ask questions of himself, Dr. Dodman, Willie or John. The questions were serious and thoughtful. When the questions period ended the entire class spontaneously stood and applauded. The educators present said they hadn't witnessed such a response before. The newspaper reporter present later acknowledged the program's success in an article in the Springfield Union-News. The article in the paper generated a request from the principal at the John F. Kennedy Middle School in Windsor, Connecticut. He asked that Willie bring Pepper Belle and the Tourette's program there.

Mountain view from the Ferrero's yard

Fall was in full swing. Large flocks of Canada geese honked support to one another as they flew south for the winter. The view from the Ferrero's yard was breathtaking. The mountains could be seen through a frame of colored trees. Bright yellow, red and deep brown leaves were sharply defined against the ultimate background of the crisp blue fall sky.

The students were encouraged to share their hobbies and special interests with the class. Betsy was telling the class about Masconette Farm. She told them a story about something that had recently happened to her. She explained to the class that she was gathering leaves behind Pepper's barn. After she gathered the leaves, she watched as squirrels and chipmunks gathered and hid nuts for the coming winter. She told the class she was startled when nine wild turkeys suddenly walked out of the adjoining cornfield headed for the underbrush. She told how she got so excited that she started to woof and scared them away. She took time to poke fun at herself by saying, "I guess they don't like dogs." She laughed with her classmates. She was learning that one way to deal with Tourette's was to talk about it rather than be ashamed of it.

Willie and Big John agreed to go to John F. Kennedy Middle school and retooled the program a little. The 600+ seventh graders gathered first on the hill overlooking the athletic field. John, in full racing colors, had Pepper hitched to her jog cart. He put Pepper through her paces. The students were again invited to get a "hands on" look at Pepper Belle. John took a lot of questions.

In the auditorium, the students were so well behaved you could "hear a pin drop." The teachers remarked about how different that type of behavior was. At the end, again the students spontaneously stood and applauded. It was as inspiring for Willie, John and Peggy as it was for the kids. John and Willie tossed about a half dozen "Pepper Belle" T-shirts to kids in the audience. Both of them wished they had a shirt for everyone.

Peggy gives a T-shirt to the new detention teacher.

The students were filing out of the auditorium as Peggy and Willie gathered flyers. One of the teachers approached Peggy and introduced herself as the new detention teacher. Then she asked if there might be one more Pepper Belle T-shirt for her son. She quickly explained that four months ago he had been diagnosed with Tourette Syndrome. She told Peggy that he was having a real tough time. Peggy told her that she was sorry and asked her to accompany her out to the car to see if there was another shirt in the trunk. Peggy rummaged through the materials and found a soiled T-shirt. She told the woman she could have it and apologized that it was a little dirty. The woman said "Thank you!" and was gone in a flash. Not however, before Peggy saw that she was starting to cry.

About a month went by and then one day Peggy got a call from a teacher from the John F. Kennedy Middle School. She told Peggy that she was the detention teacher Peggy had found the Pepper Belle T-shirt for. She told Peggy how grateful she was for it. Peggy, recalling whom the woman was, listened to her as she started to sob. "I'm sorry, but I just had to tell you how much easier you have made life for my son. The Pepper Belle program educated everyone about Tourette Syndrome." She could say no more except "thank you" again and hung up.

Peggy relayed the conversation to Willie and both had lumps in their throats. It made them both feel good that they had helped this boy. It seems destined that Pepper Belle would spend her life helping kids. Perhaps soon she might become a mother herself.

Betsy continued her friendship with Pepper Belle. She visited daily and did her chores on her free days. She had learned to live with Tourette Syndrome and was now looking forward to graduating from eighth grade and beginning high school.

Life at the Masconette Farm continues in a cycle of breeding, breaking and racing Standardbred horses. Willie is about to retire and Big John is taking over.

The End.

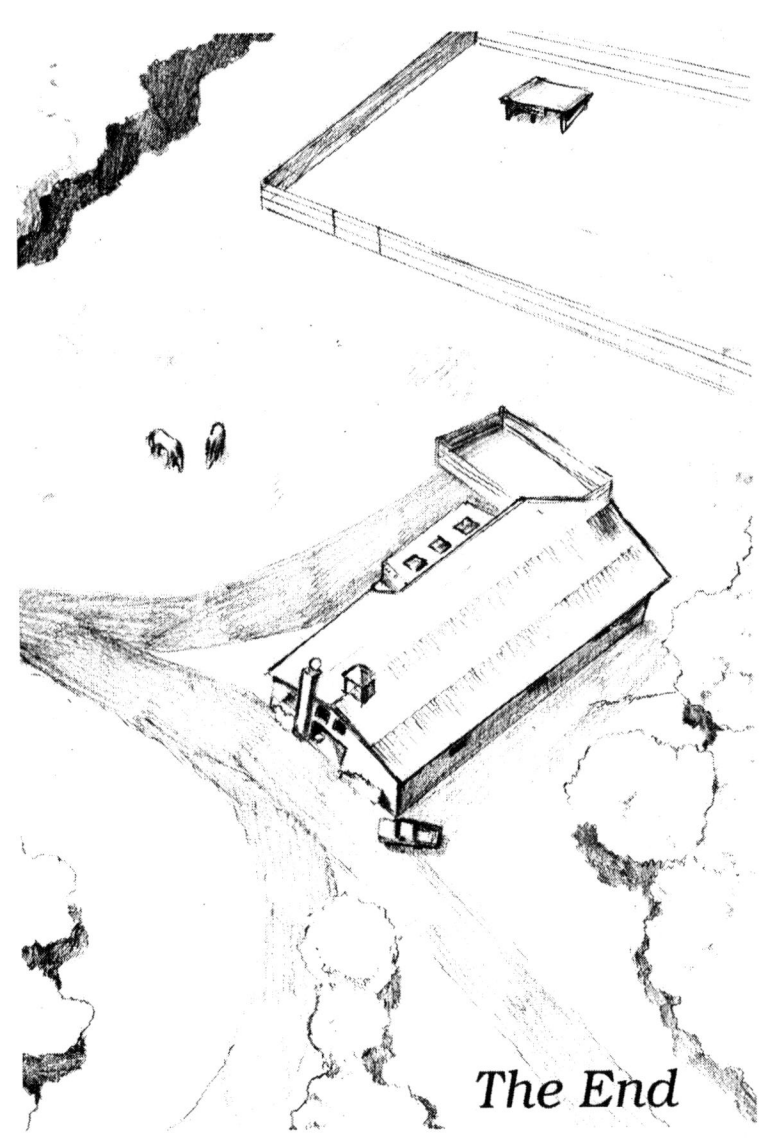

BVG